10·C·

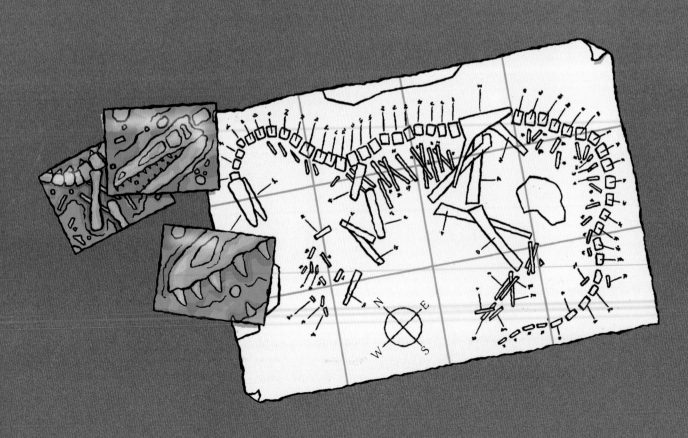

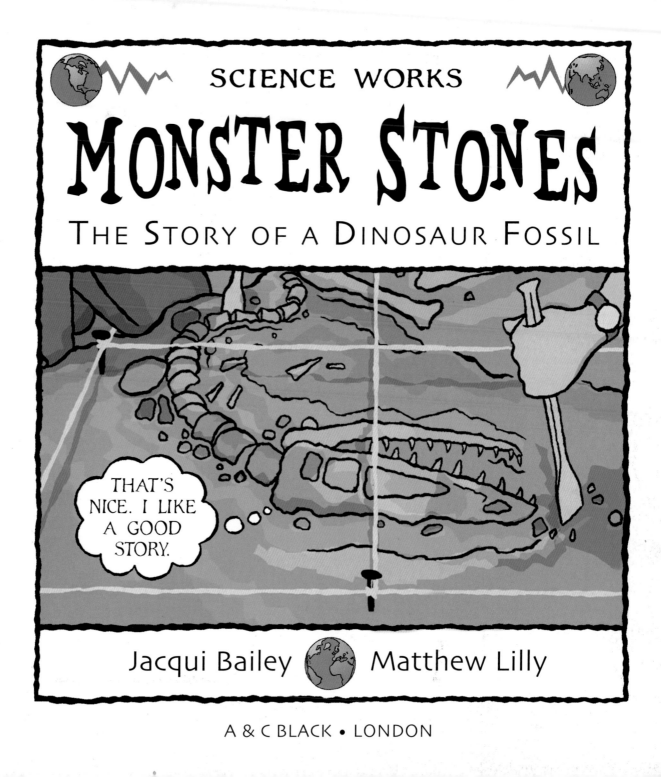

SCIENCE WORKS

MONSTER STONES

THE STORY OF A DINOSAUR FOSSIL

THAT'S NICE. I LIKE A GOOD STORY.

Jacqui Bailey   Matthew Lilly

A & C BLACK • LONDON

Millions upon millions of years ago, a dinosaur wandered by the edge of a river.

ALL I WANT IS A NICE FAT FISH OR A JUICY LIZARD.

The dinosaur was hungry. It hadn't caught anything in days.

OH YES! MINE ALL MINE.

As it stalked through the bushes, it saw a lizard sitting on a rock up ahead.

The dinosaur pounced . . . and missed. The rock began to wobble.

It crashed down the bank into the water — and the dinosaur went with it.

The dinosaur lay on the river bed and all kinds of fish, crabs and other creatures came to feed on its body.

The soft bits that didn't get eaten rotted away. In the end, all that remained were its teeth and its bones.

The gently flowing river water brought sand and mud that covered the bones like a thick blanket.

And there the dinosaur stayed.

As the years went by, something strange happened.

The dinosaur's bones began to turn into stone.

HUH?? WHAT'S GOING ON?

How? Well, it goes something like this.

A piece of bone feels smooth and solid, but if you look at it through a microscope, you will see that the bone is really full of tiny holes.

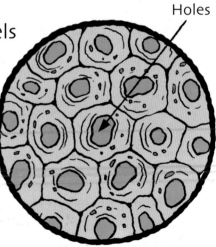

Holes

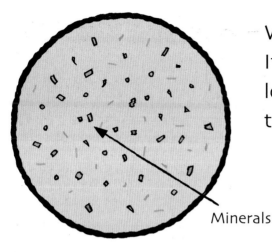

Minerals

Water isn't always what it seems either. It might look clean and clear, but it can have lots of bits of solid stuff in it, called minerals, that are too small to see.

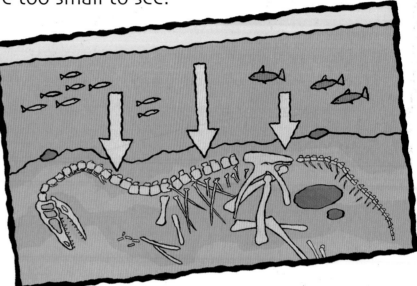

As our dinosaur lay on the river bed, the river water soaked right through its muddy blanket and into its bones.

The minerals in the water slowly filled up all the holes in the bones. Some parts of the bones rotted away, and the minerals filled up those gaps, too.

Eventually, most of the bony material was replaced by minerals and the bones had turned into stone.

More and more layers of sand and mud piled on top of the dinosaur bones.

Each layer added more weight, which pressed down on the sand and mud underneath until they hardened into rock.

Millions of years went by.

Up above, things changed. The river dried up and disappeared, and all the dinosaurs died.

Grass and trees grew where the river had been, and different kinds of animals wandered about.

Things changed below ground, too. Very, very slowly, over the years, the layers of rock were pushed upwards.

SOMETHING MOVED... I'M SURE SOMETHING MOVED.

Did you know that the surface of the Earth is always shifting about? Sometimes huge pieces of land crash into each other, and when they do, parts of the land can be scrunched up into huge folds — making mountains.

Wind and rain, snow and ice wore away at the layers. The dinosaur bones came closer . . . and closer . . . to the surface.

One wintery afternoon (after a particularly bad rainstorm), two passing hikers noticed an odd-looking stone.

The rain had washed some of the soil away, and the odd-looking stone was sticking out of the ground.

The hikers picked it up and took it home.

They showed it to a friend who worked in a museum. The friend was a palaeontologist (*pall-ee-on-tol-o-jist*).

Palaeontologists love odd-looking stones. She got very excited.

THIS ISN'T ANY OLD STONE, IT'S A DINOSAUR FOSSIL!

Fossils are bits of ancient animals or plants that have (usually) been turned to stone. They may be thousands or even millions of years old.

The word "fossil" comes from the Latin word *fossilis*, which means "dug up".

Fossils are often found buried in rock. Palaeontologists are scientists who dig up fossils and study them to find out what life was like a long time ago.

The palaeontologist found out where the dinosaur fossil came from and set off with a team of helpers to see if she could discover any more.

THIS IS GOING TO BE GOOD. I CAN FEEL IT IN MY BONES.

The first job was to dig away the top layer of soil to find out how many fossil bones were there.

Then the fossil bones were carefully chipped out of the rock, using hammers and chisels. Everyone had to work slowly as fossils are easily broken.

Sometimes the rock surrounding a fossil was scraped away with small knives and dirt was brushed off with toothbrushes.

Magnifying glasses were used to see where the rock ended and the fossil began. It took weeks and weeks.

The helpers took loads of photographs and made lots of notes about where each fossil was found.

They even drew a map of how the fossils lay together in the ground.

Then each fossil was lifted out of the ground.

Large fossils were wrapped in protective bandages soaked in wet plaster, which dried into a hard shell. Smaller fossils were packed in plastic foam and put in boxes.

The helpers labelled everything to show what it was and where it had been found.

I THINK I'M GOING TO BE SICK!

At last, the fossils were loaded onto a truck and driven off to the museum.

At the museum, the wrapped-up fossil bones were put in a storeroom — along with lots of others.

They were all waiting for a scientist to study them. Some fossils had been there for years!

One day, the fossil bones were taken to the museum laboratory. The plaster coverings were cut away and the fossils were soaked in chemicals to strengthen them.

Then the palaeontologist and her team began the long job of chiselling and drilling away bits of rock still left around the fossils. They had to be careful not to chip the fossil itself.

In really tricky places, such as inside the skull, they used dentist's drills, metal toothpicks and even needles to get the rock out.

THIS IS MORE LIKE IT.

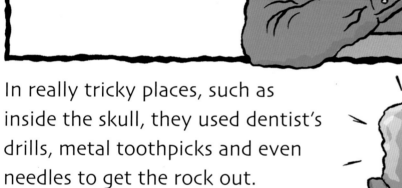

Last of all, they polished the fossil bones until they shone.

Next, the palaeontologist took more photos and made careful drawings of the fossil bones.

She would use them in her report when she wrote about the dinosaur and how it was found.

She compared her fossils with ones that had been found before. This helped her to work out what type of dinosaur the fossils belonged to.

HEY! IT'S UNCLE BILLY.

Finally, all the fossil bones were fitted together. It was hard to know which bits went where. To help her, the palaeontologist used the map and the photographs of how the fossils had looked in the ground.

The fossil bones were wired together to keep them in place.

Now the fossil dinosaur is on display in the museum. People come from all around to look at it, and wonder at a fabulous creature that walked the Earth 220 million years ago.

MORE GREAT STUFF TO KNOW

Not all fossils are made of stone . . .

FROZEN SOLID

I'LL CATCH MY DEATH OUT HERE.

In the far north, in icy-cold places such as Alaska and Siberia, much of the land is frozen all year round.

Sometimes, plants and animals are buried in ice and they may stay there for thousands of years.

People have even dug up whole woolly mammoths — skin, flesh and all — that died and were frozen 40,000 years ago.

TAR BABIES

Then there are animals that fell into lakes of sticky, black "tar" or asphalt.

The lakes formed about a million years ago, when oil from deep below the ground bubbled up to the surface. Rainwater collects on top of the tar, but any animal that tries to drink from the lake gets stuck and is sucked down. The tar then stops the animal's body from rotting away.

Hundreds of whole animal fossils have been found in tar pits, from frogs to sabre-toothed tigers.

ALL I WANTED WAS A DRINK OF WATER!

FOREVER AMBER

I GUESS I'M STUCK HERE THEN.

The sticky endings don't stop there. Some pine trees produce a gluey juice called resin. If insects, or even small tree frogs or lizards, walk in the resin, they get stuck and are caught there forever.

As the resin dries, it hardens into a glassy stone called amber. Millions of years later, the amber might be found with a perfect fossil animal still trapped inside it.

BITS AND BLOBS

Sometimes, all a palaeontologist finds is a fossil of something an animal left behind, such as its eggs or footprints — or even its poo!

Fossil poo is called coprolite and palaeontologists like nothing better than digging up dollops of the stuff. That's because coprolites contain tiny pieces of ancient food — plants or bits of bone. Scientists study coprolites to find out what sort of food the animal that left the poo ate. This also tells them what plants or other animals were alive at the same time.

TRY IT AND SEE

LASTING IMPRESSIONS

Some fossils are just copies of something that was once living. Say an animal bone, a shell or even a leaf becomes trapped in rock.

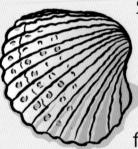

Strong chemicals called acids may dissolve it, leaving just a shape or impression of it in the rock. If the shape then fills up with a different type of mineral, a copy or model of the original object is made.

Here's how to make some "fossil" models of your own. Remember to label them!

You will need:
- Plaster of Paris
- Plasticine or play dough
- Thin card and sticky tape
- Something to use for your fossil shape — a shell, leaf, small bone, small plastic toy, even your hand!

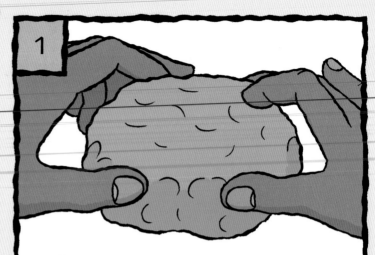

Roll out a piece of plasticine. It must be thick enough and wide enough for you to press your object into it and have a bit of space around it.

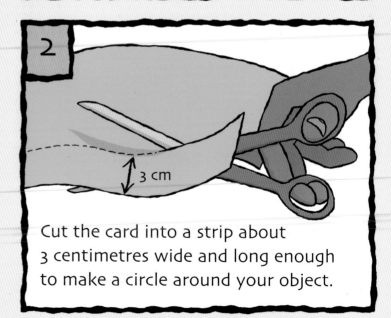

3 cm

Cut the card into a strip about 3 centimetres wide and long enough to make a circle around your object.

3 Tape the ends of the card circle together and push it gently into the plasticine base. Now press your object firmly onto the plasticine, then lift it up again. You should be able to see a clear shape or impression of the object in the plasticine.

4 Mix the plaster of Paris into a fairly runny paste and pour it over the shape until the card circle is about two-thirds full. Then leave it somewhere warm and dry to set.

5 When the plaster is hard, peel away the card and the plasticine base. There's your "fossil". You can leave it like it is, or paint and varnish it if you like.

FABULOUS FOSSILS

The oldest fossils we know of are about 3,500 MILLION years old! They look like large white circles in the rocks. They were made by the bodies of bacteria — tiny life forms that are too small to see just with our eyes. For millions of years, bacteria were the only living things on Earth.

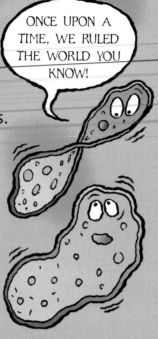

> ONCE UPON A TIME, WE RULED THE WORLD YOU KNOW!

The oldest dinosaur fossils found so far are about 230 million years old. For hundreds of years, people thought dinosaur fossils were the bones of dragons and other magical monsters.

Some fossils aren't even dead! There are a few types of plants and animals in the world that haven't changed at all for millions of years. They are called "living fossils", and they look just the same now as their millions-of-times-great great grandparents did.

One of the most famous living fossils is a grumpy-looking fish called a coelacanth (*see-luh-kanth*). Its relatives first swam in the seas 400 million years ago (long before the dinosaurs appeared).

> YOU'D BE GRUMPY TOO IF PEOPLE KEPT CALLING YOU A FOSSIL!

INDEX

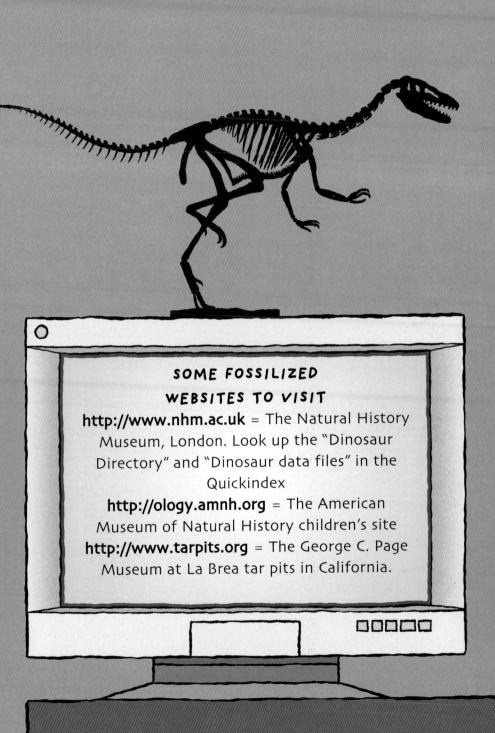

acids   26
amber   25
bacteria   28
bones   7, 8, 9, 10, 11
coelacanths   28
Coelophysis   22
coprolites   25
dragons   28
fossils   13, 26
   cleaning fossils   18-19
   digging-up fossils   14-17
   displaying fossils   21-23
   frozen fossils   24
   living fossils   28
   oldest fossils   28
   studying fossils   20
   tar-pit fossils   24
making mountains   11
minerals   9, 26
palaeontologists   13, 14,
   19, 20-21, 25
sabre-toothed tigers   24
woolly mammoths   24

SOME FOSSILIZED WEBSITES TO VISIT

http://www.nhm.ac.uk = The Natural History Museum, London. Look up the "Dinosaur Directory" and "Dinosaur data files" in the Quickindex

http://ology.amnh.org = The American Museum of Natural History children's site

http://www.tarpits.org = The George C. Page Museum at La Brea tar pits in California.

For Nick
JB

For Sarah and Peter
ML

First published in 2003 by
A & C Black Publishers Limited
37 Soho Square London W1D 3QZ
www.acblack.com

Created for A & C Black Publishers Limited by
two's COMPANY
Copyright © Two's Company 2003

The rights of Jacqui Bailey and Matthew Lilly
to be identified as the author and the illustrator of this
work have been asserted by them in accordance with
the Copyrights, Designs and Patents Act 1988.

ISBN 0 7136 6251 4 (hbk)
ISBN 0 7136 6252 2 (pbk)

Printed in Hong Kong by Wing King Tong

A & C Black uses paper produced with elemental chlorine-free
pulp, harvested from managed sustainable forests.